By MADELYN ROSENBERG

How to Behave
at a
DOG SHOW

Illustrated by HEATHER ROSS

KATHERINE TEGEN BOOKS
An Imprint of HarperCollins Publishers

*F*or my parents, and for everyone whose
pets are the best of the best
—M.R.

*F*or Gizmo McCartney
—H.R.

Katherine Tegen Books is an imprint of HarperCollins Publishers.

How to Behave at a Dog Show

Text copyright © 2015 by Madelyn Rosenberg. Illustrations copyright © 2015 by Heather Ross. All rights reserved.

Manufactured in China.

www.harpercollinschildrens.com

ISBN 978-0-06-227927-9

The artist used Photoshop to create the digital illustrations for this book. Typography by Martha Rago

15 16 17 18 19 SCP 10 9 8 7 6 5 4 3 2 1

❖

First Edition

First, you fill out the form:

Happy Tails Kennel Club

Proudly Presents

The Sixteenth Annual Best of Breed Dog Show

Sponsored by **Sloppy Kisses** Dog Food

"You'll get lots of kisses when Sloppy's in their dishes!"

OFFICIAL ENTRY FORM

Name of Dog: Rexie

Age: three and three quarters

Breed: ?

Special Skills: Tail wagging

Handler: Julia Fitzgerald and Charles

Owner: Julia Fitzgerald and Charles, too

Next, you locate the dog
and gather the supplies.

You must fill the bathtub . . .

. . . and locate the dog again.

That's not soap, Charles!

Sigh. You must hope the judge thinks

Rexie is a Bluetick Coonhound.

If you're going to be a real dog handler, you must put on a proper outfit . . .

. . . and locate the dog again.

There's no time to dig a hole

or play fetch—*especially* if you're fetching the McKagan brothers.

If you see a skunk,
you must hold your nose and
walk backward *very quickly*.

That goes double for you, Rexie.

You must refill the bathtub
and find the tomato juice.
Hurry, Charles!

Grape juice won't work.
Neither will lemonade.

Humph. You must hope the judge thinks Rexie is a rare,
strangely scented, purple-spotted Dalmatian.

You must *run* to the competition.

A grand entrance is optional.

It's best to do the final grooming
just before you enter the ring.

That hair dryer is for dogs, Charles!

The McKagan brothers are NOT beauty experts!

It's a DOG show,
not a FROG show!

When it's your turn to face the judges,
you must stand very straight
and pretend not to hear when
one of them says, "P.U."

To be a good handler, you should
use a firm but quiet voice, like this:

Sit, Rexie.

THAT'S NOT SITTING!

Stay, Rexie.

THAT'S NOT STAYING!

You mustn't become too friendly
with the competition!

Do not nibble the judge's pants!

Or steal his loafers!

The seesaw is for DOGS ONLY, Charles!

Come, Rexie.

Rexie? COME BACK!

That isn't part of the obstacle course!

You don't *need* any more shoes!

You're not supposed to—

You must apologize to the judges and gracefully accept their decision.

You must ride home with your chin in the air . . .

and an idea in your head:

You must host a dog show of your very own!

Julia + Charles Fitzgerald

Proudly Present
THE FIRST ANNUAL

BEST of the BEST
pet extravaganza
entry form

Name of Dog ___Rexie___
Age ___3 and three quarters___
Breed ___?___
Special Skills ___Digging, tail wagging,___
skunk chasing, bathtub escaping, pants eating

Handlers ___Julia + Charles Fitzgerald___

Owners ___Julia + Charles Fitzgerald___

You and I will do the judging, Charles.

After we play on the seesaw

(and after Rexie takes *his* kind of bath).

Maybe the McKagans are beauty experts, after all!

Rexie is an expert, too.
At digging!
Just look at that form!

And he's first-rate at
fetching broken sticks,

and old shoes,

and new friends.

THIS WAY TO
KYLIE'S PARTY

You're right, Rexie.

Staying is overrated.

Show us how you can run!

And jump!

And sing!

AR-AR-ROOOOOOOOOOOOOO!

The contestants must wait patiently as we make our final decision.

We must prepare the awards . . .

. . . and locate

the dog one last time.

Use these sticks
for the drumroll, Charles.

May I have the
envelope, please?

And the grand champion of the First Annual
Best of the Best Pet Extravaganza is . . .

Shhhhhhhh . . .

Sweet dreams, Rexie.